Toni Biscotti's Magic Trick

Toni Biscotti's Magic Trick

Written and illustrated by
Caroline Merola

Translated by Sarah Cummins

First Novels

Formac Publishing Company Limited
Halifax, Nova Scotia

Originally published as *La magie de Tonie Biscotti*
Text copyright © 2006 Sarah Cummins
Illustration copyright © Caroline Merola

Formac Publishing Company Limited recognizes the support of the Province of Nova Scotia through the Department of Tourism, Culture and Heritage. We acknowledge the financial support of the Government of Canada through the Book Publishing Industry Development Program (BPIDP) for our publishing activities.

Formac Publishing Company Limited acknowledges the support of the Canada Council for the Arts for our publishing program.

Library and Archives Canada Cataloguing in Publication
Merola, Caroline
[Magie de Tonie Biscotti. English]
      Toni Biscotti's magic trick / Caroline Merola ;
      illustrated by Caroline Merola ; translated by
      Sarah Cummins.

(First novels ; 60)
Translation of: La magie de Tonie Biscotti.
ISBN-10: 0-88780-719-4 (bound)
ISBN-13: 978-0-88780-719-0 (bound)
ISBN-10: 0-88780-715-1 (pbk.)
ISBN-13: 978-0-88780-715-2 (pbk.)

        I. Cummins, Sarah II. Title. III. Title: Magie
        de Tonie Biscotti. English. IV. Series.

PS8576.E7358M3313 2006   jC843'.54   C2006-904385-X

Formac Publishing Company Ltd.   Distributed in the United States by:
5502 Atlantic Street   Orca Book Publishers
Halifax, Nova Scotia, B3H 1G4   P.O. Box 468 Custer, WA
www.formac.ca   USA 98240-0468

Printed and bound in Canada

Table of Contents

For Isabelle, the little pixie

1
A Daring Move

What was she thinking? What thunderbolt hit Antonietta Biscotti that morning? Why, oh why, had she rashly volunteered to be in the school talent show?

She didn't have to! Only five or six students in her class decided to take part. But now it was too late to back out. Her teacher, Mr. Zuckerman, had written her name on the list.

Antonietta could not dance or sing. She didn't play a musical instrument. Sometimes in the schoolyard, she would imitate cartoon characters, and that would always crack up Rachel and Yousra, her best friends.

But she would never do anything so silly in front of her class. Especially not in front of the cool, the wonderful, the fabulously handsome Marco Pirelli!

Marco Pirelli! *He* was the reason

Antonietta had acted so rashly.

When Mr. Zuckerman asked the class, "Who would like to be in the talent show on December 15?" Marco Pirelli was the first to raise his hand. So Antonietta, who always had her eyes trained on him, immediately and eagerly raised her hand even higher.

With no thought at all for the consequences.

***

At recess, Rachel and Yousra were very impressed by Antonietta's daring. Yousra was beside herself with excitement.

"You are so brave, Toni! I would never dare to do a thing like that."

And she held her face in her hands.
"All alone onstage in front of
everybody. I would faint dead away!"

"Gee, thanks, Yousra!" said
Antonietta crossly. "Thanks for all the
encouragement!"

"Well, anyway, Toni, what are you
going to do? Are you going to sing,
or what?"

"That's the problem," Antonietta

sighed. "I have no idea."

Rachel, who had been listening to the conversation quietly, finally spoke up.

"I think you should do a magic show."

"A magic show?" Antonietta was confused. "I know nothing about magic!"

"Ask your grandmother. You're always telling us she's a real sorceress!"

2
The Sorceress

It was true. Nonna Maria was a bit of sorceress. Not the kind who turns children into toads or brews up magic potions. But she did have strange powers.

For example, she could read minds. If one of her three granddaughters ever told a lie, she could tell right away.

And most of the time, she knew what the truth was.

Even more strange was that Nonna Maria could see through walls. Without looking, she always knew what was happening in any room.

One day, Antonietta's little sister Clara was about to pour sugar into the goldfish bowl. Nonna Maria called out to her to stop that nonsense immediately.

Clara could not believe it!

"How did you know, Nonna? You were downstairs, I was upstairs, and the door was shut!"

Even Olivia, Antonietta's older sister, was in awe of their grandmother's powers. One day, she had decided to wear her pretty purple miniskirt, which was very shiny and very short. When her grandmother saw her about to go out, she shot her a disapproving look.

"You're not dressed like a young lady, Olivia. You're dressed like a trapeze artist! And trapeze artists sometimes come crashing down. Remember that, *bella mia*."

Olivia wore her purple skirt anyway. But her whole day was filled with petty annoyances and bad luck.

She forgot her homework assignment on the bus. She tripped on the last step and fell flat on her face in front of Andy, the cutest guy in the whole school. And she lost her little gold bracelet.

Ever since, she was convinced that her grandmother had put a curse on the skirt. She never dared to wear it again.

But Antonietta got on splendidly
with her grandmother.

As the middle child, Antonietta
wasn't really close to either sister.
Her big sister was too old, and her little
sister was too annoying.

Her parents both worked long hours.
So most of the time, Antonietta
confided in her Nonna Maria.

And that's what she did that
evening. They talked about love and
magic.

"You know, Nonna, I think I acted too quickly. I'm going to ask Mr. Zuckerman to take my name off the list. I can't do anything for the talent show."

"Antonietta, *bella ragazzina*, you acted out of passion, and I like that. Do you know what I think? This might be an opportunity to get Marco to notice you."

Antonietta was intrigued. "How, Nonna?"

"Well, by being on the same team as him."

"Nonna! We hardly even say hello once a month! This year, he's in my class, so that's good. But he isn't very interested in me."

Antonietta sighed. "He is so cute.

Well, you know that. You've seen him
sometimes, at the corner. He has such
nice eyes! And his hair is so adorable,
the way it sticks up. I wish he liked
me! I would like to impress him.
But I have no talent, my grades are
only average...."

Nonna Maria knitted her brows as she thought it over.

"Well, in that case, *ragazzina*, you have to put on such a fabulous show that Marco will be dazzled. You can do it! I'll help you, if you like."

Antonietta hesitated. But all she really wanted was to have Marco notice her.

"Maybe you're right, Nonna. And I have a month to get ready."

So her mind was made up. She would put on a magic show the likes of which no one had ever seen.

That night Antonietta had a strange dream. She turned pebbles into cookies and her friends into birds. She flew out of the classroom window and nobody could catch her.

Not even Marco.

3
A Little White Lie

To learn something new, you need the proper information.

On Saturday morning Antonietta was first in line when the doors opened at the library. But unfortunately, the library had only two books about magic. Two crummy little books that explained easy tricks that even a two-year-old could do.

As she walked over to the adult section, Antonietta stopped short.

Her cheeks flamed red and her heart went boom! There, at the end of the row! The boy in the red coat, with tousled hair. It was Marco!

"This would be a perfect time to go up and talk to him," thought Antonietta. "On the other hand, he looks like he's concentrating hard on something. I wouldn't want to disturb him."

Marco must have felt someone was looking at him, because he turned his head. When he saw Antonietta creeping toward him like a mouse, he was a bit surprised.

"Oh, uh … hi Antonietta. How are you?"

"Oh, I … yeah. Hi, Marco. Are you working on your act, too?"

"What? Oh, no. I'm just looking for

a book to read."

Antonietta felt her heart thudding in her chest. Finally! Marco was speaking to her! And he had said more than two words!

"What are you going to do for the talent show, Marco?"

"I'd rather not say. I want it to be a surprise. In any case, it's going to be good!"

"Well, I'm going to put on a magic show. Real magic. Not just tricks."

"Come on! There's no such thing as real magic. It's all tricks!"

"Of course there is real magic! You'll be amazed!"

Marco and Antonietta stood there for a few more moments, neither one knowing what to say.

"Well, yeah, so long, Antonietta."

"Bye, Marco. See you on Monday."

Antonietta felt as light as a butterfly. If she had her way, she would be dancing in the aisles of the library!

Was it possible? Had she really just had a conversation with Marco Pirelli?

Suddenly, she remembered what she had said. Had she said she was going to do real magic? Well then, she was a real idiot! She had bragged about her act because she wanted to impress Marco. And now she was trapped in her lie.

Poor Antonietta!

4
Antonietta's Hidden Talent

When she got back home, Antonietta
told her grandmother what had
happened.

"I'm so depressed, Nonna!
I couldn't find any interesting books,
and Marco must think I'm crazy!"

She hung her head in despair.

"Now, now, *bellina*. If anything,
Marco must think you are intriguing.

And you showed you were interested
in him. Men are always proud when a
beautiful woman is interested in them.
And anyway, how can he be so sure
there is no such thing as real magic?"

Nonna smiled mysteriously. She got
up and opened one of the doors of the
cabinet and took out a large book.
Its leather cover was cracked and split,
but the gold letters still shone.

"I was wondering what you could
do, too, Antonietta. Then I remembered
this book. My uncle Eduardo gave it to
me when I was your age. This is a book
about magic. The last chapter is very
interesting. It gives the secrets of
amazing magic tricks."

Antonietta was in a fever of
excitement. She opened the book on

her lap and carefully turned its pages.
It had beautiful old engravings.

"But Nonna, this book is in Italian!

I can't read it!"

"We'll study it together, *ragazzina*. I'll help you put together your act. And believe me, it will impress Marco!"

***

Antonietta set to work. Every evening, she practiced the hand movements her grandmother taught her.

"Look at me, *bellina*. You have one innocent hand, the one the audience is looking at. And while they're looking, your other hand, the guilty hand, is secretly doing the work."

Nonna Maria was very skillful, but Antonietta surprised herself. She learned quickly, and was soon adding little personal touches.

After three weeks, she could pull a dozen brightly coloured necklaces out of an empty box. Wooden buttons turned into silvery jewels in her clever fingers.

"You see?" said her grandmother.

"You thought you had no talent,
but you are more talented than I am,
ragazzina!"

Every day after she had finished her
homework, Antonietta practised and
practised some more. At the dinner
table, she would slyly make a fork or a
piece of bread disappear.

One week before the talent show,
she presented her magic act to her family.

The four members of the audience
were expecting a nice little amateur
show. They were bowled over when they
discovered what Antonietta could do.

Even Mr. Biscotti, not someone to
give a lot of compliments, raved about it.

"Antonietta, my girl, you are a real
artist!"

"My goodness, yes!" said her

mother. "She has inherited her
grandmother's gifts!"

"Toni, do that thing with the jewels
again," begged Clara.

"How do you do it?" Olivia
wondered. "Explain it to us!"

"Never. A magician never reveals her secrets."

***

Now the talent show was only three days away. After school, Antonietta wowed her friends with a few simple tricks. She was saving the more difficult ones for the show on Friday.

"Toni, tell us how you do the trick with the queen of hearts!" cried Rachel.

"Toni, I'm hungry," joked Yousra. "Make a pizza appear!"

"And a chocolate bar," added Rachel.

Suddenly Yousra pointed to the soccer field.

"Look, there's Marco! Put a spell on

him, Toni, so he'll come over here and
kiss you!"

The three girls laughed loudly.

Ah, Marco! thought Antonietta. *If
you only knew the trouble I go to for you!*

As luck would have it, at that very moment Marco turned his head and looked straight into Antonietta's eyes.

5
The Big Day

The night before the show, Antonietta was struck with stage fright.

"You know, Nonna, if I blow it, everyone in the school will laugh at me. And Marco…"

Her grandmother interrupted her.

"How could you blow it, Antonietta? You will thrill everyone, just like you thrilled your family and your friends. Come here. I have something for you."

She took something red and shiny

from her pocket and placed it in
Antonietta's hand.

"Listen to me, *ragazzina*. I am
giving you something very precious.
My uncle Eduardo gave me this golden
brooch on his deathbed. The ruby in the
centre has magical powers."

Antonietta was stunned. "Magical
powers?"

"Yes. It will protect you and give
you confidence. Sometimes it may
grant you your wish. But you must

only use it for good. I'll lend it to you for tomorrow."

Antonietta kissed her grandmother.

"Oh, thank you, Nonna! Now I know that tomorrow will be a good day. Thank you!"

"Yes, it will be a good day, my little pixie. You'll see."

**

Finally, Friday morning arrived. It had snowed all night and was still snowing.

In the schoolyard, the children waited with excitement. The talent show would start after recess.

Antonietta had put everything she needed in a box. She saw Mario walk past carrying a big duffle bag.

What kind of act was he going to do?

Finally, the long-awaited moment arrived.

The children filed into the gymnasium and noisily settled into their metal chairs. The principal, Mr. Flowers, stepped onto the stage to introduce the first performers.

Antonietta and the other performers waited eagerly in the wings for their turn.

Some kids had brought musical instruments. Ahmed Amari and Matthew Campano were dressed as clowns. Katie Prentice had on a fabulous red-and-black dress. She was going to dance the flamenco.

Antonietta was so nervous that her stomach hurt.

I should never have volunteered to

be in the talent show! she thought.
*I could be sitting happily in the gym
watching. Marco's not here. I wonder if
he's had second thoughts.*

She nervously fingered the sparkling

brooch pinned to her chest. It was comforting to have it with her.

One after another, the children went onstage to present their act. Most sang a song or recited a poem.

Antonietta held her breath. Soon it would be her turn.

Suddenly, a strange figure appeared at the end of the corridor. The children all turned to stare.

From the front, he wore a splendid wolf costume and a mask with pointy ears.

Another mask covered the back of his head, the face of a man with a big moustache. Was he a hunter? A wooden pistol hung from his belt.

As he walked past Antonietta, the half-wolf, half-hunter looked her in the eye. "Hi, Antonietta! Good luck with your magic!" he said in a friendly whisper.

It was Marco! Antonietta was so surprised she blushed.

"Oh hi, Marco! Your costume is great! Is it —"

She didn't have time to finish her question. The kids from her class were on next.

6
Showstopper

Matthew and Ahmed were the first ones on. They improvised part of their act, and they had the audience rolling in the aisles. Katie danced very well, although there were some technical problems with her recorded music.

Next was Marco. He strode to the middle of the stage, stopped, and stood there looking out at the crowd.

He seemed a little lost. Seconds passed. The audience was getting restless.

Suddenly Antonietta understood! Marco couldn't remember his lines.

Antonietta pressed her grandmother's brooch against her heart.

"Marco, Marco," she murmured urgently. "Remember your lines! This is my dearest wish. Come on, little brooch. Work your magic!"

At that very instant, Marco collected himself and began to speak. He acted

both parts. Facing the crowd, he was the wolf. When he turned his back, he became the hunter. The two met in the forest and exchanged insults. Then they began to fight.

The crowd loved it. It really seemed as if there were two characters onstage. At the end, the wolf and the hunter became friends. It was a simple story, but magnificently performed! The teachers were all impressed. The hall rang with applause.

Antonietta thought Marco was even more wonderful than she did before. However, she had no time to adore him. The principal was introducing the next performer:

"Now here is Antonietta Biscotti and her magic show!"

Antonietta bravely rolled her little table with all her accessories onto the stage. Her stomach didn't hurt anymore. Now that she knew the ruby had real magical powers she had nothing to fear.

She began, always remembering her grandmother's words: "You have one innocent hand, and one guilty hand."

She wasn't the least bit nervous now, but focused. Her hands moved with astonishing speed. She was heartened by the cries of "ooh!" and

"ah!" from the audience.

Silk scarves spun in the air.
Necklaces popped out of the little box
like magic, sparkling in a rainbow of
bright colours.

Antonietta stepped off the stage and
into the audience. She pretended to find

all kinds of strange objects in people's pockets: a screwdriver, a teaspoon, a thimble.

Everyone laughed when she pulled the principal's watch from Mr. Zuckerman's pocket.

At the end of her act, Antonietta made a bouquet of origami birds appear

out of nowhere. The audience was thrilled, and they clapped and clapped. The little kids moved closer, trying to see better.

Antonietta's face was pink with bliss. She had never felt prouder and happier.

She just hoped Marco had seen her whole act. Antonietta looked all around the gym, but she couldn't see him anywhere.

7
The Magic of the Heart

After her triumph, Antonietta went back into the wings.

There he was! Marco was standing with some friends. He took off his mask and smiled at her.

Antonietta gathered her courage and went over to him.

"Hi, Marco. I … I just wanted to congratulate you! Your sketch was great! Did you make the costume yourself?"

"My dad helped me, but it was my idea. Did you really like it? You know, at the beginning, I couldn't remember

my lines. I was panicking!"

"Really?" Antonietta lied politely. "I didn't notice."

"Luckily, it all came back to me, like magic!"

Antonietta was hoping Marco would compliment her on her act, but instead his friends jumped in.

"Your act was brilliant, Antonietta!"

"It was great! You are a real magician! How did you learn?"

"Oh, that's a trade secret," said Antonietta mischievously.

Marco gently touched her arm.

"Antonietta, I just wanted to tell you …" he said, pulling her aside. "Your act was amazing! I was really impressed!"

"Thank you, Marco."

"Uh ... It wasn't real magic, was it?
It was tricks, right?"

"Maybe," Antonietta smiled,
touching her grandmother's brooch.
"But that doesn't mean there's no such
thing as real magic."

"Anyway, Toni, you were the best. I think we were the two best ones."

Antonietta blushed all the way up to her ears. *He called me Toni! For the very first time!*

Marco and Antonietta were too

interested in their conversation to notice their teacher walking by. Mr. Zuckerman smiled to himself. He had suspected for some time that those two were made for each other. *The artistic temperament,* he said to himself.

That night, it took Antonietta a long time to fall asleep. All the wonderful events of the day kept swirling through her head.

When she finally dozed off, she dreamed once again that she was flying out one of the windows at school. But this time, Marco was flying with her.

And nobody could catch them.

More new novels in the *First Novels Series*!

Maddie's Big Test
Louise Leblanc
Illustrated by Marie-Louise Gay
Translated by Sarah Cummins
It's time for the big math test at school, and
Maddie's worried. Then her friends show her how
she can cheat...

In this story, Maddie learns that taking the time
to study can be a lot simpler than cheating.

Toby Laughs Last
Jean Lemieux
Illustrated by Sophie Casson
Translated by Sarah Cummins
When Toby climbs too high in a tree to rescue a
kite, he tumbles to the ground and has to go to
hospital. The doctors stick tubes down his throat
and bandage him up. Toby is happy to be alive —
but then he realizes that he can't laugh any more.

In this story, Toby finds out just how important
it is to be able to laugh.

Formac Publishing Company Limited
5502 Atlantic Street
Halifax, Nova Scotia B3H 1G4

Orders: 1-800-565-1975
Fax: 902-425-0166
www.formac.ca